SAMMY SPIDER'S FIRST SUKKOT

Sylvia A. Rouss

illustrated by
Katherine Janus Kahn

To my family and friends, who are a constant reminder that God is everywhere.
—S.A.R.

To Robert, who is the little boy in all my books.
—K.J.K.

OUT SIDE

KAR-BEN PUBLISHING
A division of Lerner Publishing Group, Inc.
241 First Avenue North
Minneapolis, MN 55401 U.S.A.
800-4KARBEN

Website address: www.karben.com

Library of Congress Cataloging-in-Publication Data

Rouss, Sylvia A.
Sammy Spider's first Sukkot / by Sylvia Rouss ; illustrated by Katherine Janus Kahn.
p. cm.
Summary: Sammy Spider learns about the festival of Sukkot by watching the Shapiro family build their sukkah.
ISBN: 978-1-58013-142-1 (lib. bdg. : alk. paper)
ISBN: 978-1-58013-083-7 (pbk. : alk. paper)
[1. Sukkot—Fiction. 2. Jews—United States—Fiction. 3. Spiders—Fiction.] I. Kahn, Katherine, ill. II. Title.
PZ7.R7622Sar 2004
[E]—dc21 2003027298

Manufactured in the United States of America
3 4 5 6 7 8 - JR - 13 12 11 10 09 08

A BOOK OF DIRECTIONS

DOWN

BELOW

Sammy Spider was sitting next to an open window inside the Shapiros' home looking at the brightly colored leaves on the big tree outside.

A busy squirrel, gathering nuts on the ground below, stopped to glance at the birds chirping in the branches high above.

The squirrel scampered up one side of the tree
and down the other.

Suddenly, Sammy heard a loud banging noise.

Josh Shapiro was holding two wooden beams while his father hammered them together.

“Mother!” called Sammy. “What are they making?”

Mrs. Spider crawled down from their web to the window below. “That’s a sukkah,” she answered. “Each fall, the Shapiros build a hut for the harvest holiday of Sukkot, like the one used by Jewish farmers long ago.”

“Can we celebrate Sukkot, too?” asked Sammy.

“Silly little Sammy,” replied Mrs. Spider. “Spiders don’t celebrate Sukkot. Spiders spin webs.”

Sammy crawled outside through the open window to get a closer look.

"Please be careful," warned Mrs. Spider, "and stay out of the way."

Sammy perched on the
windowsill and watched.

Mrs. Shapiro came outside carrying large cloths. She held them up while Josh and his father attached them to the beams to make the sukkah walls.

Then Mr. Shapiro climbed up a ladder and placed thin wooden slats across the top of the sukkah. Josh handed his father tree branches to cover the slats.

Sammy crawled inside the sukkah. Above him, he could see patches of blue sky. Below him, Josh was helping his mother carry a table and chairs into the sukkah.

Sammy wished he could build a sukkah, but remembered his mother's words, "Silly little Sammy. Spiders don't celebrate Sukkot. Spiders spin webs."

Josh ran into the house and returned with a large shopping bag. He emptied it onto the table.

Sammy saw bright red apples, green pears, and bunches of purple grapes. Mrs. Shapiro cut pieces of string for Josh to tie around the fruit.

Mr. Shapiro moved the ladder inside the sukkah, so he could attach the fruit to the branches on the roof.

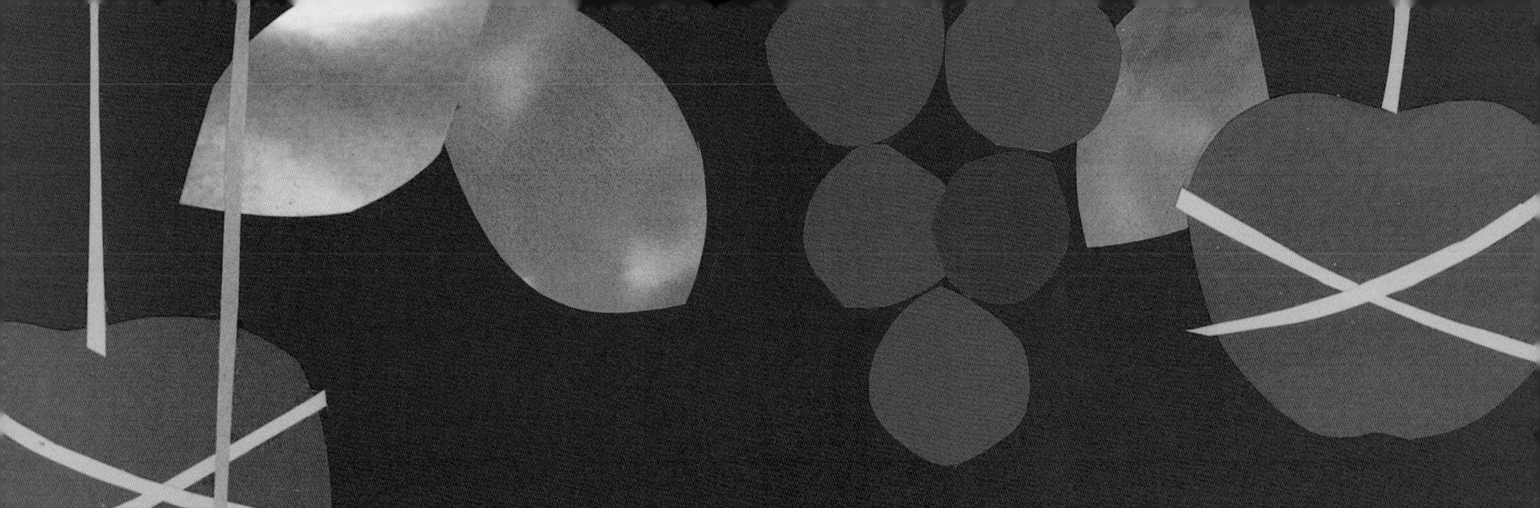

Watching from above, Sammy wanted to join the fun. He came down on a strand of webbing and crawled onto an apple. The apple swung back and forth. Sammy giggled.

Josh dashed into the house and returned with paper, crayons, and tape. Sammy watched him make a sign. "Welcome to our sukkah," Josh said as he wrote the words.

"He's talking to me!" thought Sammy, but then he remembered, "Spiders don't celebrate Sukkot. Spiders spin webs."

Josh taped his sign inside the sukkah. Sammy scurried back to the windowsill.

Mrs. Spider came outside to look for Sammy. Just then, the window slammed shut.

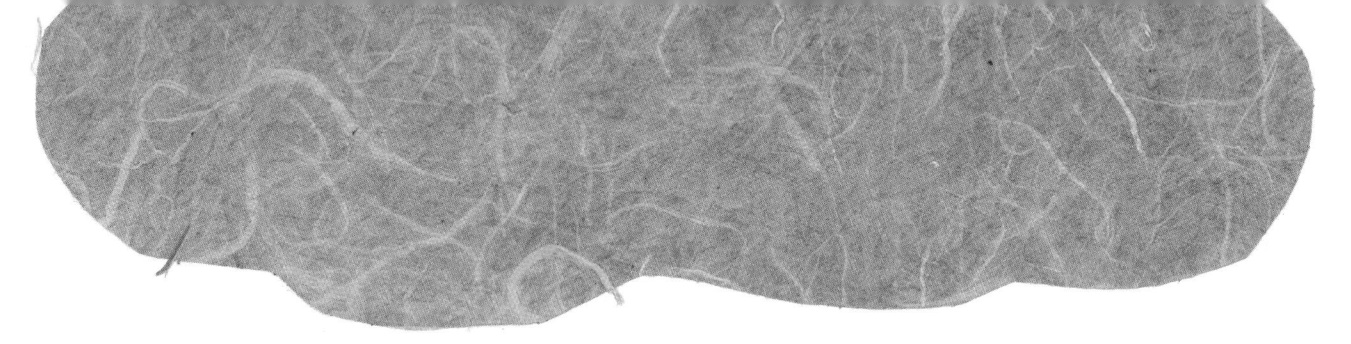

"Oh no!" she cried. "Where will we stay until we can get back into the house?"

"Inside the sukkah!" exclaimed Sammy.

Mrs. Spider followed Sammy up to the top of the sukkah. "Let's spin a web below these branches," he suggested. Mrs. Spider agreed.

The sun was setting when the Shapiros came back to the sukkah with candlesticks, a kiddush cup, and trays of food.

Sammy watched them recite the
blessings and eat their meal.

When they finished, they cleared the table and carried the empty plates back inside the house.

"Now would be a good time for us to go back indoors too," suggested Mrs. Spider.

“But the stars are so beautiful. Can’t we sleep inside the sukkah?” pleaded Sammy.

“All right,” agreed Mrs. Spider. She helped Sammy snuggle into the web. Soon they were fast asleep under the twinkling stars.

The next morning, Josh came outside to the sukkah.

"Mother, what is Josh carrying?" whispered Sammy.

"The yellow fruit is an etrog," explained Mrs. Spider. "The three branches are called a lulav. Together they remind us of all growing plants."

Sammy slid down a silky strand and crawled between the branches of the lulav.
He smelled the etrog.
It smelled sweet.

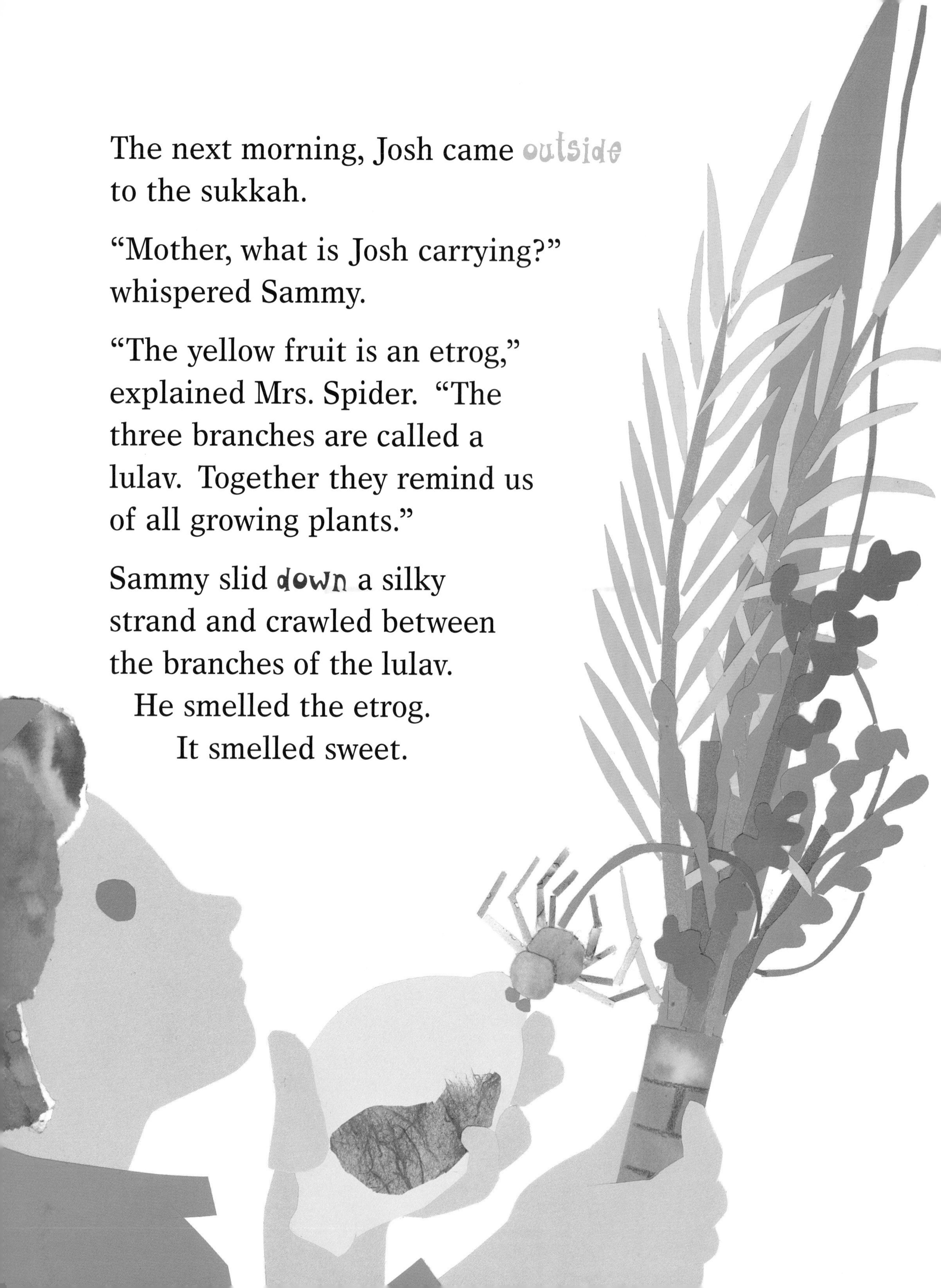

Mr. Shapiro handed the lulav and etrog to Josh. "You say a blessing and shake it in all directions to show that God is everywhere," he explained.

Sammy looked all around him.

Inside the sukkah, he was surrounded by beautiful branches and tasty fruit.

Outside, the sun was shining on the big tree with its colorful leaves.

Above were the blue sky and
white puffy clouds.

Below Josh and his family were reciting
blessings for the harvest holiday of Sukkot.

Sammy looked up and saw
his mother smiling down at him.

"Yes, God is everywhere,"
said little Sammy.